THE LEGEND OF
SLEEPY HOLLOW

by Washington Irving

retold by Blake A. Hoena
illustrated by Tod Smith
coloured by Dave Gutierrez

LIBRARIAN REVIEWER
Katharine Kan
Graphic novel reviewer and Library Consultant

READING CONSULTANT
Elizabeth Stedem
Educator and Consultant

www.raintreepublishers.co.uk
Visit our website to find out
more information about
Raintree books.

To order:
☎ Phone 0845 6044371
🖹 Fax +44 (0) 1865 312263
📧 Email myorders@raintreepublishers.co.uk

Customers from outside the UK please telephone +44 1865 312262

Raintree is an imprint of Capstone Global Library Limited, a company incorporated
in England and Wales having its registered office at 7 Pilgrim Street, London, EC4V 6LB –
Registered company number: 6695582

Art Director: Heather Kindseth
Graphic Designer: Brann Garvey
Editor: Laura Knowles
Originated by Capstone Global Library Ltd
Printed and bound in China by Leo Paper Products Ltd

ISBN 978 1 406 22491 7 (hardback)
15 14 13 12 11
10 9 8 7 6 5 4 3 2 1

ISBN 978 1 406 22497 9 (paperback)
15 14 13 12 11
10 9 8 7 6 5 4 3 2 1

British Library Cataloguing in Publication Data
A full catalogue record for this book is available from the British Library.

CONTENTS

INTRODUCING . . .

Brom

Ichabod

Katrina

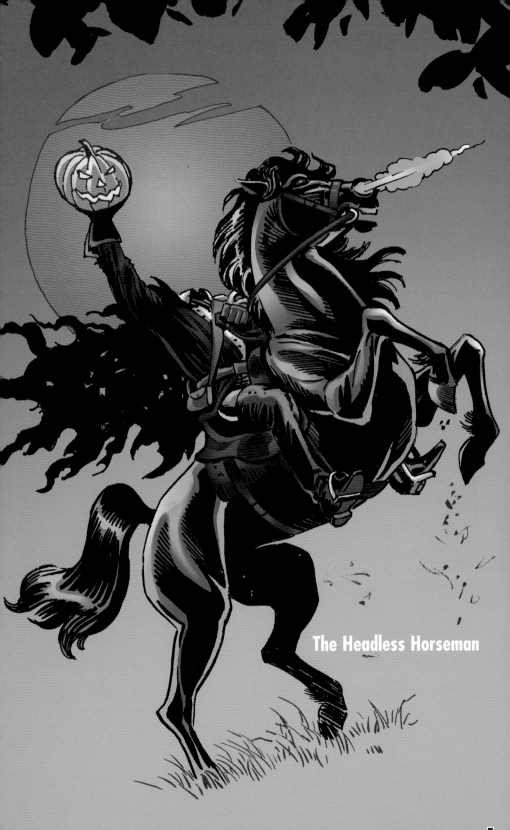

The Headless Horseman

CHAPTER 1
THE SCHOOLMASTER

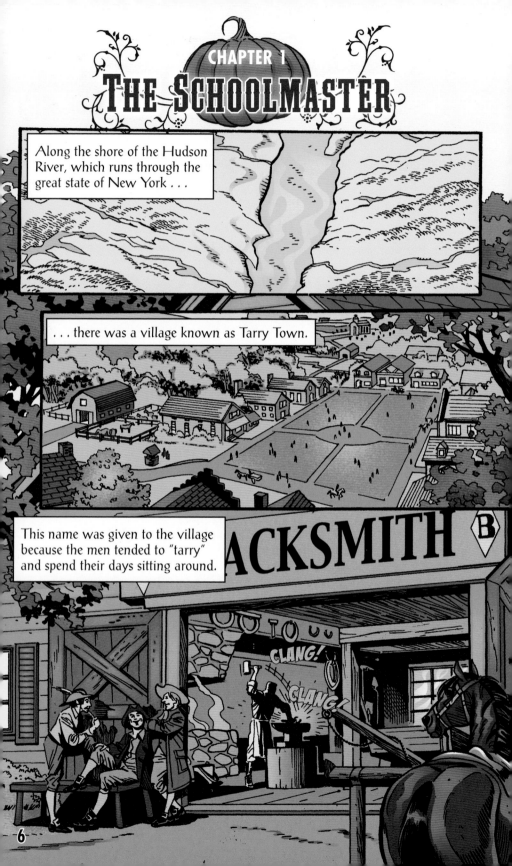

Along the shore of the Hudson River, which runs through the great state of New York . . .

. . . there was a village known as Tarry Town.

This name was given to the village because the men tended to "tarry" and spend their days sitting around.

ACKSMITH Ⓑ

CLANG!

CLANG!

Not far from the village was a little valley known by the name of Sleepy Hollow.

Tucked in one end of the Hollow was a modest farm owned by Hans Van Ripper and his wife.

They had been given the duty of boarding the local schoolmaster, Ichabod Crane.

I hope he had enough to eat.

If he didn't, I'll have to squeeze more eggs out of my chickens.

Along the edge of the Van Rippers' land stood a one-room schoolhouse.

See, there he is, boys. Right on time.

Later that day, as darkness filled the Hollow, Ichabod headed back to the Van Rippers' farm.

At night, the peaceful valley seemed like a very different place.

Shooting stars streaked across the sky and strange sounds echoed through the valley.

Local legends said the region was haunted by all sorts of ghosts.

But the most frightening spirit in Sleepy Hollow was a horseman with no head.

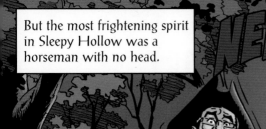

NEEEIIGGHH!!

Is somebody there?

But after dinner . . .

I would like to learn about this Headless Horseman.

That's no story to be told in front of the children.

But have you heard of the Woman in White?

Why no, I haven't.

"Many years ago, a blizzard took hold of Sleepy Hollow in its icy grip."

"Snow piled up, waist deep in some places."

"Near Raven Rock, a young woman was caught in the storm."

"Unable to find her way home through the blinding snow, she fell and froze to death."

Now during blizzards, her screams can be heard across the Hollow. The Woman in White warns travellers of dangerous storms.

Oh my!

Besides being schoolmaster, Ichabod gave singing lessons to the church choir. His favourite student was the daughter of a wealthy farmer, Balt Van Tassel. Her name was Katrina.

People often wondered if Ichabod gave Katrina private lessons because of Balt's wealth . . .

My dear Katrina!

. . . or his daughter's beauty.

CHAPTER 3
THE FINAL JOKE

A few days later . . .

Now class, this is a picture of the human brain.

The brain, of course, controls the rest of our body. Without it, our bodies would not work.

Meanwhile . . .

33

Ichabod spent the next hour getting ready for the party.

Then he set off for the Van Tassels' farm.

And don't forget what happened to old Brouwer . . .

"One night down in the Hollow, the Headless Horseman snatched him up and tossed old Brouwer on the back of his horse."

"Once they reached the bridge near the church, the Horseman turned into a skeleton."

SPLASHH!

"He threw old Brouwer into the river and flew off over the trees."

Daredevil would have beaten his horse.

"But as we crossed the bridge near the church, the Headless Horseman disappeared in a ball of fire."

BOOOOOM!

By the way, who was this person Brouwer that the old gentlemen talked about?

Brouwer? He was our last schoolmaster.

Ichabod had hoped to tell Katrina of his love for her, but . . .

. . . it was not to be.

Disappointed, Ichabod got on his steed and headed back down into Sleepy Hollow.

CHAPTER 4
THE HEADLESS HORSEMAN

That black night, Ichabod was greeted by the strange sounds . . .

. . . and unusual sights that were common in the Hollow.

MOOAAAANN!!

Ichabod was not alone.

Frightened, Ichabod tried to make Gunpowder move faster.

The Horseman!

The Horseman followed close behind.

Hurry! Hurry! Move it!

As Ichabod sped up, so did the other rider.

Then, as the rider crested a hill . . .

IT'S THE HEADLESS HORSEMAN!!

Then Ichabod saw what the Horseman carried.

Just then, Ichabod saw an opening in the trees up ahead.

He saw the bridge where Brom said the Headless Horseman had disappeared.

If I can only reach that bridge.

I am safe!

The men continued to search along the banks of the deep, black river, but the body of the schoolmaster was never found.

The following spring, Brom married Katrina. The happy couple completely forgot about the missing schoolmaster.

But others in the valley of Sleepy Hollow continued to wonder about Ichabod's fate.

He probably just up and left, embarrassed by losing Katrina's love.

I still say it was the Headless Horseman that carried him off.

ABOUT THE AUTHOR

Washington Irving was born in New York City on 3rd April 1783, towards the end of the Revolutionary War (1775-1783). This was a war faught between Great Britain and 13 of its colonies in North America. The colonies won their indepedence and went on to form the United States of America. Irving's parents named him after George Washington. In 1809, Irving wrote his first book, *A History of New-York from the Beginning of the World to the End of the Dutch Dynasty*. This book poked fun at local history and politics. Irving wrote many other satires, humorous stories that commented on people's beliefs and politics. Two of his most famous short stories are "The Legend of Sleepy Hollow" and "Rip van Winkle." Irving became one of America's first authors to make a career as a writer, and he is considered the father of the American short story.

ABOUT THE RETELLING AUTHOR

Blake A. Hoena has a Masters of Fine Arts degree in Creative Writing. Recently he's written a series of graphic novels about space alien brothers, Eek and Ack, who are forever trying to conquer Earth in bizarre ways.

ABOUT THE ILLUSTRATOR

Tod Smith studied Cartoon and Graphic Art at university. He started working in comics in the 1980s, and has been an illustrator for comics and books ever since. He loves to play music in his free time, and when he was at school, the Beatles inspired him to begin playing the guitar.

GLOSSARY

appetite desire or craving, often for food

bewitched haunted by a spell or curse

board provide someone with food and a place to stay

crested reached the very top of something, such as a hill

gravity invisible force that pulls objects towards Earth's centre

Hessian German soldier hired by the British to fight the American colonists during the Revolutionary War (1775-1783)

steed horse, especially a large, powerful one

superstition belief in supernatural things, such as magic and ghosts

tarry linger or wait around and do nothing

traitor someone who is disloyal to his or her country or government

THE STORY BEHIND
SLEEPY HOLLOW

Washington Irving is best known for writing "The Legend of Sleepy Hollow". He was also a biographer and historian. He liked to use real places, people, and events as the basis for his fictional stories.

Tarrytown lies along the eastern bank of the Hudson River, about 40 kilometres north of New York City, in the United States. Irving actually spent the final years of his life living there. Today, there is also a small village called Sleepy Hollow just down the road from Tarrytown.

The church that Ichabod walks by on his way into Tarrytown is the Old Dutch Church of Sleepy Hollow. Built in 1685, it is one of the oldest churches in New York. Where the Headless Horseman was said to be buried is the Old Dutch Burying Grounds, next to the church. A nearby bridge crosses the Pocantico River.

Irving may have based his characters for "The Legend of Sleepy Hollow" on people he met and knew in the area. Many Van Tassels lived near Tarrytown. Eleanor Van Tassel Brush, the beautiful niece of Catriena Van Tassel, is said to have been Irving's model for Katrina. The local blacksmith, Abraham Martling, may have been the inspiration for Brom Bones. "Brom" was often a nickname for someone with the name Abraham.

The character of Ichabod Crane could have come from several sources. Irving probably borrowed the name from a soldier, Colonel Ichabod Crane, whom he met while serving in the army. Jesse Merwin, a schoolteacher from nearby Kinderhook, was a friend of Irving's and may have been the basis for Ichabod's character.

The capture of Major John André that was mentioned in "The Legend of Sleepy Hollow" was an important event during the Revolutionary War. On 23rd September 1780, three local militiamen captured Major André in Tarrytown. He had made a plan with Benedict Arnold, and André's capture prevented an attack on the fort at West Point. Major André was convicted as a spy and later hanged.

There's also an actual legend about a Hessian soldier who was found in Sleepy Hollow. The Hessian was killed by soldiers of the Continental Army, and his head was nearly cut off. The legend says a local couple, out of respect for the Hessian, buried him in the Old Dutch Burying Grounds because a Hessian soldier had once saved their baby. Irving may have stumbled across this legend while working on a biography of George Washington, and it could have become the basis for "The Legend of Sleepy Hollow".

DISCUSSION QUESTIONS

1. Towards the end of the story, some of the villagers from Tarry Town wonder what happened to Ichabod Crane. What do you think happened to him? Explain your answer using examples from the story to support your answer.

2. Ichabod Crane seems to enjoy listening to ghost stories, yet on pages 30 and 31, he explains why certain ghosts cannot exist. Why does Ichabod act this way? Why does he like ghost stories, yet is afraid of the ghosts in Sleepy Hollow?

3. Washington Irving wrote "The Legend of Sleepy Hollow" as a satire, a humorous story that commented on the lives of people living in that area of New York State. Why do you think people now view it as a scary story?

WRITING PROMPTS

1. Do you have a favourite ghost story? Write it down.

2. At the end of the story, a new schoolmaster comes to Sleepy Hollow. Write a story about what happens to him. Does he encounter the Headless Horseman or another ghost?

3. Imagine that you lived in Tarry Town. Write a story about an encounter you would have with one of its many ghosts.

OTHER BOOKS YOU MIGHT ENJOY

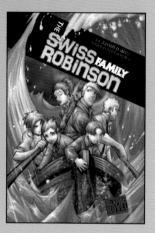

The Swiss Family Robinson

While on a voyage across the sea, a family from Switzerland is shipwrecked on a deserted island. To survive, the Robinsons must find food, water, and build a shelter. Soon, they discover that the island is filled with plants and animals they've never seen before. Unfortunately, not all of the creatures are friendly.

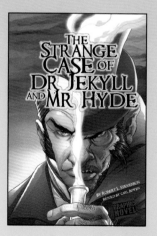

The Strange Case of Dr Jekyll and Mr Hyde

Scientist Dr Henry Jekyll believes every human has two minds: one good and one evil. He develops a potion to separate them from each other. Soon, his evil mind takes over, and Dr Jekyll becomes a hideous fiend known as Mr Hyde.

Dracula

On a business trip to Transylvania, Jonathan Harker stays at an eerie castle owned by a man named Count Dracula. When strange things start to happen, Harker investigates and finds the count sleeping in a coffin! Harker isn't safe, and when the count escapes to London, neither are his friends.

The Hound of the Baskervilles

One evening, Sir Charles Baskerville is attacked outside his castle in Dartmoor, Devon. Could it be the Hound of the Baskervilles, a legendary creature that haunts the nearby moor? Sherlock Holmes, the world's greatest detective, is on the case.

GRAPHIC REVOLVE

If you have enjoyed this story, there are many more exciting tales for you to discover in the Graphic Revolve collection...

20,000 Leagues Under the Sea
The Adventures of Tom Sawyer
Alice in Wonderland
Black Beauty
Dracula
Frankenstein
Gulliver's Travels
The Hound of the Baskervilles
The Hunchback of Notre Dame
Journey to the Centre of the Earth
The Jungle Book
King Arthur and the Knights of the Round Table
The Legend of Sleepy Hollow
Robin Hood
The Strange Case of Dr Jeckyll and Mr Hyde
The Swiss Family Robinson
Treasure Island
The Wizard of Oz